FATE

The beginning

By
Emily Pretlow

Fate *The beginning*

copyright © May 2010
by Emily Pretlow

ISBN13: 978-0-9845746-0-5
ISBN: 0-9845746-0-3

Published by -
Adventure Express Publishing
Colorado, USA

www.adventureexpresspublishing.com

Contents

Chapter 1

The Library

It is the first day of school for Elizabeth and her first fear is that no one would like her, but that all changes when she goes to the Old Creek library. She and her class go on a field trip to the library.

No one is allowed to even touch a book because they are ancient artifacts.

Elizabeth was walking around a bookshelf when she saw something sparkle so she separated from the group, went toward it; it was a book that read, "Elizabeth's Soul Book."

She grabbed it just before a set of skinny withered fingers did.

She flipped to page one and it told everything that has happened in her life like the time when her teacher criticized her report and called it wimpy.

"What is this? I never told anyone about these incidents!" She turned to page 99 and read:

6/18/2010
Great wolf attack!
Elizabeth's mom has died of a large bite

Elizabeth slammed the book closed and heard her class coming. She ran out into her line cradling the book in her backpack.

Her friend whispered, "Where have you been?"

Elizabeth said, "I've been in a section called Ghosts, because I love ghost stories."

"Okay." Her friend said.

Later that night, Elizabeth read some more the book and she fell asleep with the book open.

All of a sudden, the book turned to page 56 and in that page, it told about a strange wolf that she dreamt before, but it felt more realistic.

She heard a howl and woke up, noticing the wolf sitting next to her, a bit of his fur got in her mouth.

She quickly tried to spit out the horrid hairball that was in her mouth. She heard the wolf speak, "We have to get out of here!"

Elizabeth said, "Why?"

"Just do it!" He snarled.

"Oh for heaven's sake, get on my back and hold on."

Elizabeth asked, "What's coming after us?"

"Something bad" he said.

"Hold onto the book because if they get a hold of it, they will not hesitate to burn and kill you."

She safely tucked it in her backpack. Soon they arrived at the wolf's den and she saw his other siblings and his cousin. Elizabeth got off the wolf's back and laid down in a bed of leaves and fell asleep.

As soon as Elizabeth was asleep, the wolf walked over to his cousin.

"Fate" she said, "do you think we should tell her?"

"Tell her what?" he asked.

"You know, G-l-e-n." she whispered.

"Oh him, why? It could scare her too much that she might run away." He whispered.

FATE

"Fate, don't you think she would want to know who we're fleeing from?" she snapped.

"Oh fine, why do I have to do the dirty work?" Fate said, under his breath.

"Elizabeth, get up. I have to talk to you!" Fate said.

"The person that we are fleeing from is called Glen; he is the leader of all the cities. He has killed many. Strange deaths have happened because of him, and you and I are the only ones that can stop him, because your soul book wasn't burned. I am warning you now, don't mess with Glen, he has spies everywhere and he can tell them at any time to kill you. Okay?"

"Yes"-said Elizabeth.

Now the reader is probably wondering, whose skinny fingers were grabbing at the book at the library?

Well the answer, they are Glen's secretary's fingers; her job is to actually get the soul books for Glen to burn.

Chapter 2
Glen's Fury

Meanwhile, Glen's secretary came in.

"Did you get it?"

"No my lord."

"Grrrr!"

"Do you know what this means?" He grabbed Deth's throat. No answer, he shook her throat and asked again.

"Yes my lord."

"Enough with you!" he threw at the ground...

Fate sensed that Glen's spies had been sent out. Fate shook Elizabeth's shoulder. She shuddered.

"Get your belongings and hop on my back. Oh, if you ever see a crow, kill it."

"Kill it! Are you insane, I love birds?" Elizabeth yelled.

"They are spies of Glen."

"Oh." Elizabeth grabbed her book, put it in her backpack, and got on Fate.

They ran for days only stopping to eat or drink and sleep. Finally, after three weeks or traveling, just over the horizon they saw a city.

Fate called it Faith City, but it was really called Draken City, which means Death City in Dragen tongue, faith was always among the town's people's spirits.

"Hurry! Get into you backpack! I'll carry you," said Fate.

"Why?" Elizabeth asked.

"Just... okay, they don't allow humans here. They'll take you to Glen and he will kill you!" explained Fate.

"But I'm too big!" whined Elizabeth.

"Okay, stand back,..." Fate stretched the seams of the bag out. Elizabeth got in.

Slowly they crept into the city and everyone began to chant, "Strong warrior! Strong warrior!"

Fate turned to the crowd saying, "Okay, enough, I have returned."

Elizabeth forgot she had some feathers and a fake beak from acting class.
She inhaled a feather through her nose and sneezed. "Oh-oh" she thought.

The crowd stopped praising Fate and started toward Elizabeth. As the crowd lurched forward, Elizabeth had to think fast.

She took the bottle of tacky glue she had from art class, glued all of the feathers to her shirt, and put on the beak.

As the crowd drew forward, Elizabeth jumped out of the bag and put on the phony rooster act. In her tank top and shorts, she looked funny.

"Who are you?" stuttered a little hen.

"Uh, I'm Robie Rooster." Elizabeth muffled out.

"Okay." The little hen said.

Just then, victory exploded inside Elizabeth, as she thought, "Yes, they bought it. I'm a disguise master, yeah!"

"Want to join me for some chicken feed?" asked a little hen.

Fate stepped on Elizabeth's foot to get her attention. He gave her a stern look, and Elizabeth knew what it meant.

"Okay," she croaked in pain.

◇◇◇◇

Soon they were at the hen house. "Hold on I'll get your plate," said the hen. The little hen soon returned with grains of chicken feed, and said, "Eat up!"

Elizabeth's stomach lurched as Fate growled, "Okay."

She ate a handful of the stuff and swallowed, as she thought, "at least it is something to eat."

"Thank you for joining me for dinner," said the hen.
"You're welcome," replied Elizabeth as she left. "Ooh, do we have to stay here again?"

"No," replied Fate.

"Yes!" -sighed Elizabeth.

"We should rest, okay?" Fate yawns
"Yeah." Said Elizabeth

Back at Glen's castle...

"Grrr, send the troop out, make them search Draken City!" Glen growled, at Deth, his secretary.

"You better get that girl or you'll be my next lunch," growled Glen at his troop of killers.

"Don't make me go out there either, or I'll slice your throats."

"Yes S-sir." said the lead crow.

Just as Fate and Elizabeth left Faith City, they encountered a crow. The crow began to crow loudly and flew away quickly.

"Oh no! Get it Fate! Get it!" screamed Elizabeth.

Fate jumped up and caught the bird in mid-air, and brought it down with a swift bite at the neck, he killed it. He tore a mouth full of the bird's breast and said, "Lunch!"

A crow that had been nearby, at the time, went back to Glen and cawed, "Our scout has been killed."

Glen's interest sparked up. "By who?" Glen growled.

"The wolf and the girl." The crow said.

"The why didn't you attack?" Glen asked, infuriated.

"I..." The crow didn't get to finish his sentence he got snapped in his master's jaws.

Glen burped up some feathers and said, "Skinny bones come here!"

After a couple of seconds, a skinny sand elf waddled over. "Yes?"

"I want you – to go over with this scale and go over to

the wolf and girl and befriend them. And I want you to report to me every night, okay?" he explained.

The little elf sighed and set off toward Draken City. The elf soon arrived shortly after he left Glen's castle.

Fate had sniffed him out long before arrived. Fate growled, "Who is there? If you don't show yourself I'll kill you!"

After Fate said that, the little sand elf slid out from behind the rock of which he was behind.

Elizabeth gasped in surprise, "What is that?"
The elf blushed to so much attention. He flitted up to fates snout and sat on it.

"Skinny Bones is my name," he said in a hushed tingly voice. He blushed again.

Elizabeth reached out to pet his tiny head, but he bit her finger.

"Ouch!" She said and snapped her finger back.

"What are you here for?" Fate growled.

"I dun' no" said the elf.

"Aww it's cute! Let's keep him!!" said Elizabeth.

"I don't know..." said Fate. "He looks like a spy..." Fate said.

"No, he is cute, he probably just got lost." She said. "Please, oh please! Can I keep him? He can sleep in my backpack, just till his owner comes back," she whined.

While Fate and Elizabeth argued, Skinny Bones held his breath waiting for his chance to spy.

"No!" snapped Fate.

The little elf jumped off Fate and unnoticeably flew into Elizabeth's backpack.

As he flitted in, his head hit Elizabeth's soul book. "It's here!" said Skinny Bones, "The great book."

Chapter 3

Discovery

When it was midnight, Skinny Bones crawled out of Elizabeth's backpack when everyone was asleep. He slowly walked past Fate. When he did, Fate snarled in his sleep. Skinny Bones jumped, but Fate didn't notice anything.

As soon as Skinny Bones was out of hearing distance, he reported to his master. Slowly his master's voice rang through the canyon.

"Do you have a lead of to where they are?" came Glen's questioning voice.

"Yes, master." said Skinny Bones shamefully.

"Well, where are they going?" said Glen.

"Oh yeah, Kraceen City." Said Skinny Bones, startled. (It is pronounced Crak-keen).

"I will be there tomorrow night and kill them and I will have a great war once again!" said Glen.

Before Glen left, he said, "And since he is fleeing toward the one place I've been looking for, for years, the

Temple of Arabic Times, where I will receive power to control this universe. But, if they get there first...," he was cut off by a deep growl from the shadows.

Piercing red eyes peered through the darkness. Out stepped a Basilisk, the most dangerous being of all. Skinny Bones hid because Basilisks eat things that don't sleep at night.

The Basilisk came out of the shadows, stepped toward Skinny Bones' hiding place and sniffed the air, growled and lifted up Skinny Bones and was about to eat him, when Elizabeth go up and threw a stone in Basilisk's eyes. The Basilisk disintegrated to a million pieces.

Skinny Bones turned around and saw that Elizabeth had thrown the stone and was the one who had saved his life from the Basilisk.

He turned and ran toward her, "Oh thank you! Thank you!" said Skinny Bones.

"Skinny Bones, you can go in my backpack if you want." Elizabeth said.

"Okay" he stuttered.

Before she let Skinny Bones in, she asked him, "Who were you talking to?

"Uh... a fish, yeah a fish. I have a special power to talk to fish," he said. (Which was really not true).

After Skinny Bones was asleep, Fate got up and sniffed

the air and he caught the scent of Skinny Bones, a crow, and a Basilisk.

"What happened here?" he thought.

As soon as Elizabeth got up, he asked her what had happened last night.

"Uh... nothing" she said.

"I smell that blasted elf again too; he was sneaking around our camp while we slept." Fate growled.

"Are you missing anything?" Fate asked.

"No nothing." She replied.

"Well okay, I just wanted to make sure that darn elf didn't steal anything." Fate said.

"Okay he didn't." Elizabeth said.

The next day in the human world; GIRL GONE MISSING, that's what the top story was on the front page of the Creek Times.

Elizabeth's parents were heartbroken and baffled.

"What happened on that night before she disappeared?" a news reporter asked Elizabeth's mom.

"Leave me alone I didn't have anything to do with this!"

her mom said.

◇◇◇◇

While Elizabeth and Fate went back to sleep, Skinny Bones got out or the backpack, called Glen, and said, "Master! I found the book; it's in the forest, hurry before they leave."

"Okay" Glen said.

Chapter 4

Attack

In the morning, Fate woke Elizabeth up and then they started moving again. While Fate and Elizabeth were walking in a dense forest, she heard a twig snap.

She turned to see who it was but nobody was there.

Just as she thought it was her imagination, a band of crows suddenly started to pour out of the forest, swarming around Elizabeth and Fate, then they all started to bore down on them...

The last thing Elizabeth saw before she blacked out was a tall figure looming over her.

Chapter 5

The Castle

Once Elizabeth woke up from her dazed sleep, she saw she was in a small cage made out of pointed pine samplings making any hope of escape gone.

The floor was sticky with sap and the overwhelming sent of pine went to her head, making her feel woozy.

Next to her Fate sat in a corner of the cage chained and muzzled to the sidebars. Awhile later, a cloaked figure came shoved some kind of mush on a plate through a little door.

"Eat." It grumbled

While the fat lumbering creature left, Fate looked at Elizabeth and Elizabeth understood what he meant, "Sorry."

She walked to toward him; at least the cage was big enough to walk in. She walked over to him and put her hand on him.

"It's okay. I'll get us out of here." She whispered in his ear.

FATE

She took a hold of the leather strap holding the muzzle to his head, yanked, pulled it, and twisted it, but it didn't break.

She gave up with a sigh and sat down. And an idea came to her, she took the leather strap and attached it to a point of a sapling and said, "Pull."

And he did and soon it snapped off and Fate was free.

As soon as they were free, they needed a plan to get out of the cage.

Fate walked by a loose branch and it snagged his fur and made a small gap in the wall, big enough to get through without notice.

That night, while the guard fell asleep Elizabeth and Fate slipped out of the camp, grabbing her soul book from the place by the fire.

When they walked by the monster grunted in it's sleep and the ancient oak chair it sat on groaned as if it could collapse at any moment.

As soon as they were out of the camp, Elizabeth heard a low growl behind her. She looked and saw Fate growling at another wolf.

Before Elizabeth could run, one of the wolves grabbed her by the shirt and ran off. Soon they came to a whole bunch of wolves.

"I've found food!" the wolf howled.

In the crowd sat Fate.

She was about to call out to him, but he shot her a warning glance not to.

A single crow sat in the middle of the crowd staring at Elizabeth's backpack. Before it could lunge at it, Fate jumped at it, grabbed it by its wings, and said, "Look, an appetizer!"

They all turned and started devouring the crow and the crow's croak was cut off.

While they devoured the fat bird, they escaped.

"That was a close one!" Elizabeth said.

"Yeah" growled Fate.

Chapter 6
Black Feathers

As soon as a horse came in sight Fate said, "Get on, ride, and follow me!"

Soon they were near Krakeen City, above them strangely shaped shadows shifted along Elizabeth.

When they got there, Elizabeth stopped dead in her tracks. In front of her and Fate were Glen and a band of crows. In the Temple of Arabic times black feathers scattered on the ground.

"Well, well, well" growled Glen, "Nice to finally meet the much talked about Elizabeth," he said.

"Now be a good girl and give the book." He growled.

"What book?" said Elizabeth.

"Don't TEST ME OR I WILL KILL YOU!" He yelled.

He yelled, "Oh, Oh-h, okay"

She handed him he soul book.

FATE

"Noooo!" cried Fate and lunged at Glen.

Glen slashed Fate's side as he jumped and let out a howl of pain and fury.

"You ignorant fool! You think you can get it back. It's all over Fate. Now I can rule this world and the next!"

Elizabeth let out a gasp of terror.

Elizabeth ran toward the forest with Fate

"How could you?" growled Fate.

"I didn't give him my book." She said.

"Yes you did! I saw you!" snarled Fate.

Elizabeth laughed and said, "I didn't give..."

She was cut off by Glen's howl of fury. "She lied! She gave me a different book!" he roared.

Fate looked at Elizabeth with confusion. He winced at his deep scar in his side and began to lick it.

Glen shouted, "Go crows, go and hunt them down and when you kill that blasted wolf and bring me the girl's book and Fate's body, I will let you feast on their flesh!"

The crows cowed in agreement and set out on the search.

Elizabeth sat down next to Fate and started to cover his wound with strips of cloth from her shirt.

He winced as she tied it around his waist.

"I'm so sorry that I got you hurt, Fate. I feel so bad and it was my fault." Elizabeth mumbled.

Well at least it made it more believable," said Fate.

Chapter 7

The Beginning of the End

Elizabeth fell asleep next to Fate only to be disturbed by Fate's whimpering.

Fate got up and said, "Elizabeth we have to get out of here."

"Why," Elizabeth asked.

"Because of the crows, Glen sent out the flying rats," growled Fate.

Skinny Bones just woke from a nap and got out without seeing Gate.

"The elf!" said Fate, in astonishment.

"What, oh no, no, don't..." Elizabeth was cut off by Skinny Bones shriek of terror! Fate lunged at him, killed him, and lapped up the blood.

FATE

by Emily Pretlow

That was the end of him.

"No, no, no!" said Elizabeth and bent down, picked up Skinnybones' head, and threw it.

After awhile Fate sat down by a fire that Elizabeth made.

She asked Fate, "So, Fate, am I the only one that can kill Glen?"

"Yes, the only way to kill a person here is to burn the soul book. And Glen wants to kill every human and be leader of the universe and stuff."

"So, why are you involved?" asked Elizabeth.

"Because in the ancient verse, I am supposed to mentor you, because of the soul book, if you learn it right, it will let you become very strong, as strong as Glen." Fate Answered.

"What's the ancient verse?" asked Elizabeth.

"Okay, here it goes." Fate let out a howl and started to growl, then said, "When a girl is to find the book, a seeker shall look forward and Glen shall be dead."

He growled again, "Here is the second part." He started to snarl.

"But with all this hard work, a great trouble will come like a shadow of her very soul, and a deliverer whose meaning is strife will tell her there is no hope. But then there will be a victory, it will have its losses and its blessings. And a wolf shall come and save her life that will be her mentor."

"Oh." said Elizabeth. "We should get some sleep." Fate yawned.

While Elizabeth and Fate slept, a ban of crow scouts passed over them, but didn't see them. A little wolf pup approached Elizabeth's backpack, grabbed her book, and ran off.

Fate woke Elizabeth up and Elizabeth gasped when she saw book was gone.

"Fate, Fate! My book, it's gone, it was stolen!" yelled Elizabeth.

Fate got up and smelled the wolf tracks. "It was a wolf cub!" growled Fate.

They follow his tracks and in three days, they found the wolf pack.

"Hey Ma, look what I found!" said the cub.
"Hush, Kana, hush"

"My book!" Elizabeth said.

Fate jumped out of the bushes and circled the pack.

"Give me the book!" he barked.

"Never!" snarled the pack.

Fate lunged forward into a flurry of claws and teeth. He

managed to bite down on the pup's tail. The leader, a grey timber wolf turned and bit on Fate's bandage.

Fate, infuriated, turned and bit his throat. The wolf fell to the ground bleeding.

Elizabeth picked up her soul book and accidently dropped a schoolbook the grass. A scout of crows soon passed over the carnage and flew back immediately, chattering excitedly.

"Master! Master! We found them and the wolf is dead!"

"Really, but how?" he growled.

"I don't know, come and —— the book!

"It is there!" they cawed.

"Yes, yes! I'm coming."

The troop reached the sight, went over to the body, and feasted on his flesh.

"You blasted fools! This is not the book!" Glen roared.

He went over to one of the crow scouts that had lied to him and he grabbed the bird and was about to kill him when Fate's scent drifted to him from the trees. Before Glen could turn around, Fate jumped on his back and bit onto the scruff of his neck.

Glen rolled on the ground helplessly, exposing his belly and throat. Fate lunged at Glen's throat as Glen gasped in surprise.

Glen lay there in the grass while the crows stared at their master. They were too shocked to see Elizabeth standing next to Fate.

"Now Elizabeth, it is time for your training on how to become stronger than Glen," said Fate.

While they went off into the forest, Glen started to twitch on the ground and his eyes opened.

Chapter 8
Training

Elizabeth had advanced well in her training and it was three weeks since the fight between Glen and Fate, and Fate's wounds had healed nicely. The only thing left of the wound is a pale scar.

Now it was midnight, Fate and Elizabeth settled down to sleep.

Around Glen's body, the birds sat, thinking about eating their master's body or not. They heard a growl and flew up in the air shocked.

Glen got up, shook his head, and growled, "Hah, Fate tried to kill me, but still I live! That shows how invincible I am now! Nobody can stop me!"

Fate woke up because he heard all the commotion in the valley and snarled, "No, no, this can't be happening, Glen didn't die!"

Fate dug a hole in the earth, put Elizabeth in it and all of her stuff, and then crawled in, hoping that the dirt masked his scent.

FATE

Glen got up and walked all over the forest thinking and searching for Fate. He stopped just outside of the den Fate had made, sniffing the ground.

"He's here, or was," growled Glen.

From the den, Fate saw Glen's white coat and ducked down so Glen could not see him. Glen ran off through the trees toward the crows' camp.

"All of you!" Glen called to the crows.

"Go to the stone crossings and find wolf and the girl, if you bring me them I will kill them, and you will have the pleasure of eating them!"

The crows set out, searched, and then settled for the night near the den Fate had dug.

Fate didn't see the crows in the gathering dusk and went out to go to the bathroom. The watch crow saw Fate and woke up his comrades.

The crows silently rose up into the air and when Fate was heading back to the den, they grabbed him and Elizabeth and took them into the air.

"Let-me-go!" Fate growled.

They flew over a waterfall, when Fate snapped at the crows' feet hanging onto him. They let go, Elizabeth fell next to Fate, tumbling through the air.

Fate kicked Elizabeth toward the water to save her life.

Fate then fell and hit the muddy bank below him with a thud.

Elizabeth fell into the water screaming, "Fate! Nooo!" She splashed into the water and then waded out and sat next to Fate's still body.

The lead crow, whose leg was severed by Fate's jaw, came to his master and Glen said, "What happened?"

"The wolf, we found him and the girl, he bit off our legs, but he fell onto the ground and is now dead," said the crow.

Glen turned and followed the crows to Elizabeth

"So we meet again, Elizabeth," growled Glen.

"Your mentor died, yes?" he said.

"Take her to the camp and supervise her and torture 'till she tells us where the Arabic Times Jewel is."

Elizabeth was sitting down and noticed that a piece of carrion was lying in front of her. She picked it up and threw it. It landed next to Glen.

Glen growled and saw his whole army of starving crows flying toward him. While Glen and the crows flew away from her, Elizabeth ran to where Fate was.

"Fate! Fate! Fate, don't leave me. Elizabeth said crying.

A faint shutter woke in Fate. "I... w-will... not...leave...

FATE

you." Fate whispered.

The next morning Fate was up and limping badly on his front left paw.

"We need to get away from here." Elizabeth said.

Fate and Elizabeth traveled hundreds of miles and finally stopped in a valley. Fate tripped on a rock, the paw he had injured had caught on it and it snapped back into place. He yelped.

"Elizabeth, there is something I have to tell you!" yelled Fate.

Chapter 9

Wolf

"What" said Elizabeth?

"With the soul book, you can turn into a wolf." Fate said,

"How?" Elizabeth asked.

"You can concentrate on being a wolf, and say 'Wolfanana.' You can also turn into a wolf a second time," Fate explained.

Elizabeth thought and thought, then turned into a black wolf with green eyes.

"Whoa, everything I see is..., better. I can see well!" When Elizabeth talked, her voice came out in growls.

"Good, now people will be less suspicious, and I can talk wolf so that will be easier." Fate growled.

"We should get going" Elizabeth snarled. "Glen and his crows will be here soon." Fate agreed.

Fate and Elizabeth soon arrived at an abandon mountain cave, sat down, and knapped.

Elizabeth dreamt, "I want to go home." She said to an imaginary person.

"No you are a wolf now, you cannot go home now." It said, "No, no, nooo." Elizabeth howled.

"Elizabeth! Elizabeth! Wake up!" Fate growled.

"What, what?" Elizabeth snapped.

"There is a wolf outside; he said he wants to talk to you." Fate said.

"Ahh, the chosen one." The wolf said in a rasping voice.

"There is no hope," he rasped and stuttered. "I'm dying. I was told to tell you... you can't beat Glen. He is too strong."

"By whom were you sent?" Elizabeth asked. But the old wolf lay dead in front of her.

Elizabeth began to shake.

"What?" Fate asked.

"The ancient verse..., it's coming true." Elizabeth gasped.

"It's okay." Fate said licking her muzzle.

"Fate, once I turn into a wolf, can I turn back into a

human?" Elizabeth asked.

"No."

Elizabeth sighed. They curled up at the end of the cave together.

"How old are you?" Elizabeth asked.

"Seventeen," Fate mumbled.

"I'm sixteen." Elizabeth said.

They fell asleep together.

The next morning Elizabeth woke up itching terribly. "I got fleas," She moaned.

Fate walked over to her and told her to groom herself. They sat down together and started grooming each other.

"Fate," Elizabeth said, "Can we go hunt, I'm ravenous."

"Yes, there is a herd of dear nearby...," Fate said.

"Can you teach me?" Elizabeth asked.

"Yes, I can feed you like a cub all the time, can I?" Fate growled.

"No." Elizabeth snapped.

They soon found the herd and a newly berthed fawn, that had a deformed leg that was at a odd angle sticking out.

Fate howled, and Elizabeth joined in to. It felt joyous for her, she felt wild and free.

The herd of deer heard them and ran. The fawn was behind the herd limping badly

Elizabeth lunged and ceased the fawn's leg, bringing him down. She killed it with a swift bite to the neck, her broad muzzle glinting with blood in the sun. They dragged the fawn back to the den and feasted on it.

"How do you like it?" Fate asked.

"It's good." Elizabeth growled. "Do you want that leg?" Elizabeth asked while reaching for it.

Fate snarled and snapped at her ear. She yelped backing off.

Later that afternoon Elizabeth thought of her parents, and what they would do if they saw her as a wolf. She started to whimper and shiver.

Fate walked over to her, nuzzled her, and licked her muzzle. "It's okay, come and sleep with me tonight, it's cold out." Fate growled.

"Okay." Elizabeth said, crawling over to him. They slept peacefully that night.

They woke with a start. There in front of the mouth of the cave stood a massive Arctic wolf, Glen.

Luckily, Elizabeth had buried her soul book in a shallow hole.

"Last night I thought a smelled a fresh kill." Glen said.

Elizabeth gulped in fear. Fate licked her face.

"It's okay; I won't let him touch a hair on your pelt." Fate whispered in Elizabeth's ear.

"May I join your pack while my birds hunt for some runaways?" Glen asked.

"Sure." Fate said.

"Good, good." Glen said.

"I'll go get another deer." Fate said.
"I'll come." Elizabeth said.

"No, you will stay!" Fate barked.

Elizabeth whimpered and tucked her tail between her legs and whimpered again.

As soon as Fate left, Glen walked over to Elizabeth and growled, "Do you want to go away with me and be my mate?"

"Uh..."

"I will love you and nurture you."

He prompted, "You can have pups, I won't mind."

"I...uh, already I am part of a pack." She said.

Luckily, a deer was outside the den. Fate heard all of the conversation and growled. "She is mine!" he said to himself. He dragged the carcass into the cave.

"Meat." was all that Glen said he went over to it and started eating.

Fate went over to Elizabeth and asked her, "Did he hurt you?"

"No." she whimpered. "Fate," Elizabeth said. "I'm scared." She whispered in his ear.

"I know, and I love you. I won't let him hurt you." He said.

"I do to, Fate." Elizabeth whimpered!

"I know." Fate said, licking her muzzle affectionately.

Elizabeth thought, "As long as I'm a wolf forever, I can love him."

The next morning Glen said, "You can go hunt, I have to use the bathroom."

"Okay." Fate said, looking at Elizabeth.

While they left, Glen nosed around in the dirt and dug up the Arabic Times Jewel. "Now I need the second jewel, that in the human world."

"Now I have to go to the Analegh cliff and speak the ancient words and then... Oh yes, I will take that black wolf and be her mate because, I will be father of the ones with powers, because the verse says that when you mate a wolf with green eyes, after you rule the world of Analegh, which I already do, the pups will behold the powers." Glen growled.

"How did those wolves get this jewel...?" He wondered.

Elizabeth was outside the den with Fate and they heard him.

Elizabeth gasped.

"I won't let him do that to you." Fate said to Elizabeth.

Fate and Elizabeth came in.

"Thanks for letting me stay." Glen said, and then left.

As soon as he was over the hiss with the crows flying, following behind him, Fate said, "We will have to fight him, it's earth's only hope," growling in desperation.

Chapter 10

Stalking Glen

They followed Glen and Glen saw Elizabeth.

"So, why are you here?" He asked.

"I was wondering if I can join you." She whimpered.
"Yes, yes. It does get lonely her now days." Glen said.

(Fate agreed with Elizabeth to stay nearby and stay in the trees).

Elizabeth was walking with Glen. "I will teach you some fighting moves, do you want to?" Glen asked.

"Okay, that's fantastic!" Elisabeth said shakily.

Glen had no idea that he was nurturing the wrong side. He was nurturing good and it thrived. He dug a shallow hole and put grass and feathers from his crows in the hole.

"There, that should be fine." Glen said and lied down with her.

◇◇◇◇

The next morning, Glen was nowhere to be seen. In front of her was a deer freshly killed and she ate it. The crows were gone too. She closed her eyes and drew in the air through her nose and smelled Glen and the scent to a nearby human city.

She saw Glen burning soul books and his vicious crows eat their fill of human flesh. Elizabeth gasped in terror.

Then she saw a wolf running toward her. At first, she thought it was Fate but when she drew nearer, she saw it was Fate's cousin.

"Hey!" Elizabeth barked.

The she wolf said, "My pups! They are coming!" she growled.

"Hurry, hurry, I have a nest!" Elizabeth snapped. Elizabeth showed her the nest.

Elizabeth turned around as she birthed. She looked at the pups and saw that they were pure white, like Glen.

"Who is the father?" asked Elizabeth.

"Glen." The she wolf said.

Elizabeth went over to the pups and gently turned them over and saw that they were both males.

"I'm going to use the bathroom, help yourself to the deer." She nodded in the deer's direction.

"Thanks for all this." Fate's cousin said.

"Fate," Elizabeth said. "Your cousin, she mated with Glen and had pups!"

"What!" Fate growled, jumping up. "Let me talk to her!" He ran over to the nest and saw the pups.

"Kene! How could you?" Fate barked and then stalked away.

Elizabeth saw over the horizon that Glen was killing Fate's family.

Fate snarled and ran toward Glen.

Elizabeth jumped on Fate and held the scruff of his neck. When he calmed down she let go—"We have to get out of here." Fate snarled.

"Fate! Fate! Oh how I missed you!" said Kene.

FATE

Fate growled and stalked away with Elizabeth.

Glen came back asking Kene, "Where is the black wolf?"

"She went away. A wolf came and got her." Kene said.

"I'll get her later." Glen said.

Elizabeth was running with Fate.

"We need an army!" cried Elizabeth.

"Yes we need to travel to Anile; it's on the other side of the Analigh cliff, where Glen's going." Fate said.

"Good we'll have an ambush for him there." Elizabeth said.

They arrived at the cliff and jumped across. A crow was there and saw them cross the bridge. They walked over to some dens and Elizabeth barked into a hole, "Anyone home?"

A snake hissed and Elizabeth backed off.

They stayed in the city and heard a low growl coming from a den nearby.

Out came an old wolf. He saw them and howled.

Three largely built wolves came out and growled. "Follow us."

They came to a field full of holes. These wolves shoved Fate and Elizabeth in one of the holes and blocked the exit with a rock.

Elizabeth whined and put her head on her paws.

"It's okay. I'll get us out of here." Fate said.

He turned around and started to dig a hole in the wall of the den. Later that day he finished digging the hole, it had a narrow passageway with a large cave, large enough to fit two mates and pups.

They were gasping for air now. They knew the sad truth; the other wolves were starving them of air.

In the morning, Elizabeth was gasping for sir. "Fate, we have to get some air!" she gasped.

She scratched at the roof of the den. She slumped down with her feeble attempt.

Fate got angry and started scratch now, and bit at the earth above them.

◇◇◇◇

"Well, we better check on our prisoners." One of the guard wolves said.

They moved the rock and went in. Fate heard them, rolled in the dirt, and hid in the corner. Elizabeth did the same.

"There not here!" roared the guard.

Fate jumped and hit the roof. The whole cave fell in, but Elizabeth and Fate escaped.

The guard wolves were buried alive. One of the wolves was snapping desperately and he bit down on Elizabeth's soul book.

"Fate, dig my soul book is in there!"

Fate began to dig. He uncovered her soul book. The other wolf held on and was drug out with it. The wolf snarled.

Fate lunged at his neck. While they fought the other wolves were trying to get them to stop, they finally managed to separate Fate and the guard wolf.

When the adrenalin calmed down Fate growled, "We need an army."

"For what?" the wolves barked.

"To fight against Glen, whoever does will be rewarded with a feast and a piece of cattle!" Fate barked.

The wolves suddenly perked up to the idea because cattle were rare in their land.

Chapter 11
Failure

The next morning they organized groups, males in groups, females in other groups.

"Now when we see Glen, attack him!"

"Do whatever pleases you; push him over the gorge, do whatever." Fate explained.

Elizabeth was the lead female for one of the groups, Fate the other.

They trained daily and shared meals. They posted guards and lookouts around the camp perimeter. The guards often fell asleep on duty, waiting for the next shift.

Back to Glen: "Yes! Yes! I found that Arabic Times power, now I can go to earth and kill humans and take over!"

FATE *by Emily Pretlow*

He gathered his crows and was giddy with excitement.

The guard wolf woke up suddenly to his surprise to see the troop of crows and Glen.

Glen began saying the ancient words to let him go to earth.

"Attack!" the guard wolf howled.

The camp got up, Fate and Elizabeth began to go toward Glen, but it was too late, he had gone to earth.

"My family, earth, my friends, I let them all down." Elizabeth said.

"No, there is still hope." Fate whispered.

Chapter 12

Earth

"It all happened so quickly." Glen thought. He looked up and saw the big towers.

"I've made it!"

Glen saw a person's big pudgy hand grabbing his fur.

"Dog patrol!" Glen turned around, furious.

"So, we have a white husky, no... a... wolf!" The human said.

Glen bit his hand, tearing through his flesh.

"They are easy to kill here!" Glen said. The human ran away, screaming like a banshee.

Glen went from human to human, killing.

"Kill, Kill, Kill!" he thought.

FATE *by Emily Pretlow*

Then he felt it, cold steel around his neck, closing like a steel jaw.

Glen reached around and bit it in two—the human went fleeing.

The next city over was Old Creek town. Elizabeth's mom stared in horror at the television. She had a new son now, 10 years old.

"I lost Elizabeth 11 years ago, and I won't lose my son, Max," she said, turning off the TV.

Max was outside playing with his neighbor's dog Fido. Max loves dogs and especially Huskies, because there a close resemblance to the wolf.

"Come on Fido!" Max shouted.

Fido came back with fur in his mouth, white fur—Glen's.

"Hey, this looks like wolf fur, cool! Probably from the zoo!" Max exclaimed. He grabbed it and rushed inside, giddy with excitement.

"Hey Mom!" he yelled. "Look at this!"

He showed his mom the fur.

"What is it?" She asked.

"White wolf hair!"

His mom gasped in horror, and ushered him into his room.

Chapter 13

A Plan

A day after Glen left, Fate woke.

"I have a plan." He said.

"There is a second jewel that only you can use; you can take me with you to earth."

Fate passed her the jewel. Elizabeth took it in her mouth.

"How do I use it?" she asked.

"You remember what earth is like and it just happens." Fate said.

Elizabeth sat down and began dreaming about her mom and dad.

Chapter 14
Home?

Elizabeth and Fate woke up in a steel webbed cage with bright lights.

"Where am I?" Elizabeth asked Fate.

"On earth." He growled.

"We came to earth last night while you were sleeping." Fate mumbled.

Max came home after school smiling, holding his report card. "All 'A's!" he yelled to his mom.

"Okay Max, we can go get a dog now." She said.

They got into their silver pickup truck and drove to the Old Creek humane center. They walked in.

"Do you any wolf like dogs?" Max asked.

"Yes, just came in today, a pair of them." The desk clerk said, leading them to Fate and Elizabeth.

"Oh! They do look like wolves." Max said.

"Let's get them." His mom said.
"Okay, let's take them out." The clerk said.

She the clerk grabbed Fate by the collar and put on a leash.

"Here's the male, and..., here's the female." She said.

"Oh I love the black one!" Max yelled.

Elizabeth looked up and saw her mom. She began to thrash madly out or Max's hands and lunged at her mom, covering her with licks.

"Okay! Okay! Down girl!" She yelled.

Elizabeth jumped down.

"By, thank you!" Elizabeth's mom yelled. She put Fate in the back of the truck.

"Hop in!" she said to Elizabeth.

She hopped onto Max's lap.

"Geeze! You smell like raw meat!" Max said.

Elizabeth turned around and growled in Max's face.

"You are a wolf." Max whispered.

As soon as they got home, the wolves went inside sniffing around.

"Fate, my soul book it's in the car!" Elizabeth barked.

They ran outside, hopped the open window, and grabbed the soul book.

"Where can I put it?" Elizabeth thought. "I'll put in my room." Elizabeth barked.

She bolted into the house, climbed the stairs and nuzzled open the door. Everything was still there. She placed her book under her bed.

"What are you doing in here?" scolded Elizabeth mom, Lilly.

"Get out, bad girl!" Lilly said, shutting the door.

She put Elizabeth and Fate outside and chained them to a wooden doghouse.

"Now what?" "We are chained outside in the blazing sun!" Fate barked.

Inside, "Hey Mom, you know the dogs we got, they aren't dogs, there wolves." Max said.

"How..., oh my goodness! They're trying to kill Oreo, our rabbit!" Lilly yelled.

Max ran outside grabbing Fate's collar.

"No!" He shouted, slapping Fate's muzzle. Fate turned on Max; ears erect, tail down and began growling. His growl rumbled out of his throat.

He yanked the chain out of the ground and stepped forward, menacingly.

"Fate, don't do it!" Elizabeth barked. Fate stopped.

"Do you even know who he is?" Fate barked.

"No." Elizabeth whimpered.

Max ran into the house brining out dusty, stinky brand food pellets.

"I'm so sorry; I forgot you were a wolf" Max said, patting Fate's head.

Fate sniffed the pellets and said, "They call this food! I call it rubbish!"

Elizabeth walked over and took a bite. She spit it out, flipped the bowl over, and started chewing on it.

Chapter 15
Glen's Terror

"I will kill you all!" Glen howled.

"Now to the next town" Glen thought.

"I need my crows!" Glen growled.

He stopped walking and let out an eerie howl.

Soon a cloud of crows came flooding down. People in their homes screamed.

"Go find Fate and Elizabeth, I know they're here!" Glen snarled at the crows.

The crows took up into the air. "Look a black wolf" said the crows, flying over Lilly's house.

◇◇◇◇

"What is that dark cloud? Get the dogs inside!" Lilly said.

"Man! They didn't eat mom!" Max called.

"Okay, give them some in here" Lilly said.

The crows soon passed over. It started raining.

Elizabeth saw Lilly cooking dinner. When Lilly looked at the news, she gasped.

Old Creek Times
Wolf Kills and Heads Towards Us!

"It all started last week," says one resident. Folks think that a white wolf has escaped from the zoo and has killed more than 500 people. Some people say it has rabies, others say a plague. Just to warn people stay inside.

We talked to the science center and they say if they manage to kill it or find it dead, it will be a scientific study.

Bob Wilson.

Mad Wolf Attack
Many die others escape maimed.
Picture by Bob Wilson

"Keep the dogs at guard," Lilly said.

"Can I give them meat?" Max asked.

"Yes! Just do it!" Lilly said.

Max let Fate and Elizabeth outside. He threw out a whole thawed chicken. Fate lunged and so did Elizabeth. They ripped it in half and ate it whole.

Elizabeth and Fate jumped the fence into the surrounding forest. Fate gnawed off his collar and Elizabeth's.

"Thank goodness!" Fate growled.

They walked around, drawing in the scents.

"Crows!" Fate barked.

The crow that saw them took off through the trees to tell Glen.

"Master! Master!" the crow squawked. "I've found them, Elizabeth's a black wolf."

"What?" Glen barked.

"Follow me," said the crow.

The crow led them to the forest. Glen began smelling the earth.

"Human!" Glen barked.

Max unfortunately was up in the tree watching Glen.

"Set up camp here!" Glen yelled.
"Where... is..., Max." Lilly said to her husband.

"I don't know." He said, watching T.V.

"Max! Max!" Lilly yelled.

Fate and Elizabeth went into an abandon fox hole. They lined the nest with feathers and hay. Fate curled up with Elizabeth and they both fell asleep.

"Wow! A white wolf, I'll stay up here and observe!" Max thought. He took out his bedroll and layed on it and fell asleep.

Glen walked around the forest. He stopped outside a fox hole and sniffed inside. "Fox." He said, and walked on.

"I know Glen's here." Fate said. He went out of the den while Elizabeth slept. He walked towards the crow camp. He gently placed one paw in front of another. He was so close to Glen he could taste it.

The crow closest to Fate opened one suspicious eye and crowed loudly. The crows started to wake up. The crows grabbed Fate and put him in a cage.

Chapter 16

Alone

Elizabeth woke up the next morning seeing that she was alone.

"Fate? Fate?" She called—no answer.

She got up and crawled through the entrance, stretching. She picked up Fate's scent.

"It's from last night, I don't need to worry." Elizabeth said. She walked around.

"Crow scent." Elizabeth said. She walked toward a bramble bush and saw a strand of white fur on it.

"Glen!" Elizabeth gasped.

She looked around and heard a nearby scream.

"I hope my mom's alright." She grimaced.

That night, when fate did not return she began to pace around madly.

"I must, I must find him." She thought.

Back in Glen's net cage..., "What are you doing?" Fate yelled.

"Preventing me from dying" Glen said simply.

"I'll say the verse again." Glen said.

"When a girl is to find the book, a seeker shall come forward, and Glen shall not be dead. But with all this hard work a great trouble will come over her like a shadow over her very soul; and a deliverer, who's meaning is strife, will tell her there is not hope. But there will be victory, it will have its blessings and its losses, and a wolf will come forward and save her life, her mentor." Glen said.

"No! That's not how it goes!" Fate growled.

Glen sat down in front of Fate and began eating. Fate looked at it with eyes glazed with hunger.

"Where is Elizabeth?" Fate asked.

"I don't know, why don't you tell me? You're practically in love. That's funny a human in love with a wolf. What do you think of that? Glen said.

Fate kicked at the bag.

"What did you make this out of?" Fate asked.

"Oh, horse hair, crow feathers, leather, snake skin, and human skin." Glen said.

"How many people did you kill?" Fate snarled.

"Oh, about a thousand," Glen said.

Fate's eyes glazed up with fear for Elizabeth.

Chapter 17

ax

"**M**ax!" Lilly called. She walked out into the woods. Elizabeth heard her and got up and look straight at her.

Max woke up the next day finding that beady-eyed vultures surrounded him.

"Go! Shoo!" he said swishing his hand. Max looked down to see Glen with a crow next to him.

"Whoa." He thought, taking a snap shot.

Lilly looked at Elizabeth, she looked back, "Bring me to Max" Lilly said.

Max was still staring at Glen when he saw a wolf in a net. "How strange" he thought.

He climbed out over the flimsy branch that was over Fate.

"It's my new dog!" he whispered.

Fate heard him and looked up, thinking, "How stupid is this boy?"

Max started to reach his hand down onto the net when he felt a piercing pain in his back. He turned around to see a red-eyed crow. He tried to grab it but it hopped out of the way.

"Stupid crow," he snarled through clenched teeth. It was at the middle of the branch now, the weakest spot.

Max flung himself toward it. Fate stared at Max dumbly.

Max landed on the branch with a thud.

"Gotcha" he said.

He let the crow free he heard a loud moan. The branch gave away and Max fell to the ground next to Glen.

Glen turned around and advanced slowly. Max stared helplessly at Glen.

"Max!" exclaimed Lilly.

That drew Glen's attention away quick enough that he could scurry up the tree.

"Fate!" Elizabeth barked.

"Don't come here, Glen! I will kill you!" Elizabeth snarled.

"Okay, I'll stay my distance," said Glen slyly.

He walked over to Max's tree and sat underneath it.

Fate nodded to Elizabeth to do the same. Her mom ran forward, "Max!" she screamed.

Elizabeth jumped forward and bit the sleeve of her shirt, bringing her down in a fluid-like movement. Elizabeth growled menacingly.

◇◇◇◇

That night Lilly sat down and dozed off. Elizabeth sat guard, playing an endless game of stare.

The next morning the tension was high.

"Momma! I'm hungry!" Max said from in the tree.

"It's all right baby," she said.

Fate poked his muzzle through the little holes in the net. He found a weak spot and started to gnaw on it.

Chapter 18
Battle Heat

The next night Lilly had a plan. She climbed the nearest tree. Elizabeth tried to stop her. Lilly climbed on the branch closest to Max.

"Max! Max!" she whispered.

Max turned around and stared with horror; behind his mom was Glen, jaws agape, teeth glistening.

"M-Mom!" he screamed.

She turned around, only to be bitten underneath her throat. She fell with a thud.

Everything was blurry, a spinning world, seeing Lilly.

FATE

Elizabeth jumped to her mom.

"Mom! Mom!" she barked. Her mom looked into her eyes and said weakly, "You are Eliza...." She shuddered and laid still.

Elizabeth muzzled her and said to Glen, "The battle has begun."

She lunged herself at Glen only to get blocked by curtain of crows.

"Elizabeth!" barked Fate, as he broke free. He lunged on Glen as he turned.

Fate grabbed Glen by the paw and turned him over, exposing his chest and belly. Just as he lunged toward his neck, Glen thrust his hind paws into Fate's belly.

Fate landed dazed into some brambles.

Chapter 19

Fate

Glen went toward Fate, but Elizabeth jumped on his back, biting his neck.

Scarlet blood began to spread over Glen's white coat. With one last attempt, he lunged at Fate, biting his collarbone.

Fate yelped and Glen dropped into the grass.

"Nooo," he said weakly.

"Fate!" Elizabeth said, with blood running in her ears.

She stood over Glen saying, "Thou shalt not kill." Then bit his throat mercilessly.

FATE

by Emily Pretlow

She ran over to Fate, dragged him out or the bushes, and laid him down.

"Fate, don't leave! This can't happen again! It can't." She whimpered, standing up and circled around him protectively.

"He is still breathing," said Elizabeth nervously.

"Elizabeth...," said Fate, barely audibly. "I will not..., n-not... die!"

She sat down next to him and fell asleep.

"Fate" Elizabeth whispered.

About the Author

Emily Pretlow wrote Fate—in 2007 at the age of nine, and is writing the next installment in the Fate series, **Battle Heat**.

She lives in Florida, loves animals, and loves to read, which inspired her to begin writing. She also likes to illustrate, but not as much as reading or writing.

◇◇◇◇

Keep howling for more!

Look for **Battle Heat** book 2 soon.